MIDDLE EAST.

withdrawn

Cockadoodle-doo, Mr Sultana!

For Heather, Olly, Rose, Holly and Daisy – M.M.
For Nan, with love – H.S.

Scholastic Children's Books
Commonwealth House, 1-19 New Oxford Street
London WC1A 1NU, UK
a division of Scholastic Ltd
London ~ New York ~ Toronto ~ Sydney ~ Auckland
Mexico City ~ New Delhi ~ Hong Kong

First published in hardback in the UK by Scholastic Ltd, 2004

Text copyright © Michael Morpurgo, 2004
Illustrations copyright © Holly Swain, 2004

ISBN 0 439 98219 7

All rights reserved

Printed in Singapore

2 4 6 8 10 9 7 5 3 1

Cockadoodle-doo, Mr Sultana!

Michael Morpurgo
Holly Swain

SCHOLASTIC
PRESS

In a far off eastern land there once lived a poor old widow. All she had was a goat for her milk, a few hens for her eggs, and a cockerel to wake her up in the mornings – a little red rooster.

The little red rooster loved his mistress very much, but he had always dreamt of going out into the big wide world and having great adventures.

cockadoodle-doo

One morning he woke up and said to himself, "Today's the day. I'll just wake my mistress up, then I'm off on my adventures."

So he crowed and he crowed, and then up he flew out over the fence, out into the countryside beyond.

"Come back, little red rooster!" cried the poor old widow. "Come back!"

But the little red rooster was never very good at doing what he was told.

"Goodbye, Mistress mine. Goodbye," he cried. And away he went as fast as he could go.

He hadn't gone far when he began to feel rather hungry. So he scratched around in the earth for something to eat, a wriggling worm maybe, or a burrowing beetle. He scratched and he scratched, but he still couldn't find anything to eat.

He did find something else though, something very pretty, that twinkled and shone and glittered in the sun.

A diamond, a precious diamond!

"Finders keepers," thought the little red rooster. "Mistress mine loves pretty things, and she's got nothing pretty of her own. I'll give it to her after I've had my adventures."

And so he picked it up in his beak and went happily on his way.

All day under the hot, hot sun he walked, until at last he came to the walls of a magnificent palace that seemed to be made entirely of shining marble and glowing gold.

Suddenly he heard behind him the sound of horses' hooves and jingling harnesses.

It was the Sultan returning to his palace from the hunt, with all his courtiers and servants.

As he passed by, the Sultan caught sight of the little red rooster.

"I am your great and mighty Sultan," he said, "your Lord and master. If I'm not mistaken, you have a diamond in your beak. That's valuable, very valuable; and what's more, it's mine. All jewels found in my kingdom belong to me. Drop it. Drop that diamond."

But the little red rooster was not frightened of anyone or anything and, besides, never much liked doing what he was told.

"I don't think so, Mister Sultana, or whatever your name is," he said.

"Mister Sultana! Mister Sultana!" roared the Sultan. "How dare you speak to me like that!" He called his servants at once.

"After him!" cried the Sultan. "Catch me that cheeky rooster!"

There was a great kerfuffle of dust and
feathers and squawking as the servants tried to
catch the little red rooster.

All around the palace walls they chased him.
But the little red rooster was far too quick for
them, and far too cunning.

"Cockadoodle-doo," he crowed. "I'm very much faster than you!"

But the moment he crowed, he dropped the diamond. The Sultan's servants grabbed it and gave it at once to the Sultan, who was delighted, of course.

"Put it in my treasure chest," he commanded, "with all my other diamonds and emeralds and rubies and sapphires."

But he wasn't going to be happy for very long. The little red rooster wasn't going to give up that easily. He wasn't like that.

That night as everyone in the palace slept, the little red rooster flew up to the Sultan's window.

"Cockadoodle-doo, Mister Sultana!" he crowed. "Give me back my precious diamond."

"How dare you wake me!" roared the Sultan. He called in his servants. "After him! Catch me that cheeky rooster!"

All night long they chased after him through the palace. The little red rooster had lots of fun. He ran. He hopped. He flew. But in the end one of the Sultan's servants crept up behind him and grabbed him by his tail feathers.

"Aha!" cried the exultant Sultan. "I've got you now! You've crowed your very last doodle-doo!"

"I don't think so, Mister Sultana," said the little red rooster.

By now the Sultan was very tired, and very angry too. He had had quite enough of this little red rooster.

"I'll teach you!" he cried. "I'll teach you. I'm going to throw you down the well," roared the Sultan. "See how you like that."

So he took the little red rooster by the neck and threw him down the well.

The little red rooster wasn't at all frightened of water. He knew what to do about that. He simply said: "Come, my empty stomach. Come, my empty stomach, and drink up all the water."

It took some time, but that's just what he did. He drank up all the water, every last drop of it. Then up he flew again to the Sultan's window.

"Cockadoodle-doo, Mister Sultana!" he crowed. "Give me back my precious diamond."

"What!" spluttered the Sultan. "You again!" And he called in his servants at once. "After him!" he cried. "Catch me that cheeky rooster!"

So the servants chased and chased the little red rooster until at last they caught him again.

"Aha!" cried the exultant Sultan. "I've got you now! You've definitely crowed your very last doodle-doo!"

"I don't think so, Mister Sultana," said the little red rooster.

By now the Sultan was really furious. "I'll teach you! I'll teach you! I'm going to throw you in the fire!" he roared. "See how you like that!"

So he took the little red rooster by the neck and ran to the stove and threw him in the fire.

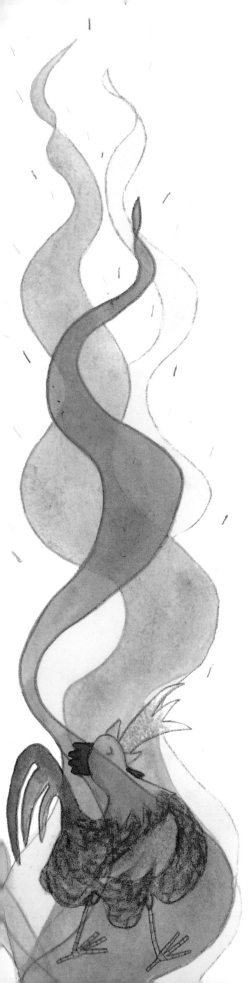

But the little red rooster was not at all frightened of fire. He knew what to do about that. He simply said: "Come, my full-up stomach. Come, my full-up stomach. Let out all the water and put out all the fire."

It took some time, but that is just what he did. He let out all the water and put out all the fire, every last spark of it. Then up he flew again to the Sultan's window.

"Cockadoodle-doo, Mister Sultana!" he crowed. "Give me back my precious diamond!"

"What!" spluttered the Sultan. "You again!" And once again he called in his servants. "After him! Catch me that cheeky red rooster!"

So they chased and chased the little red rooster until they caught him again.

"Aha!" cried the exultant Sultan. "I've got you now! You've definitely, definitely crowed your very last doodle-doo."

"I don't think so, Mister Sultana," said the little red rooster.

Now the Sultan wasn't just angry. He wasn't just furious. He was hopping mad. Like a crazed camel he was, like a vengeful vulture.

"I'll teach you. I'll teach you," he roared. "This time I'm going to throw you in the beehive! See how you like that!"

So he took the little red rooster by the neck and threw him into the beehive.

But the little red rooster wasn't at all frightened of bees. He knew what to do about them. He simply said to himself: "Come, my empty stomach. Come, my empty stomach and eat up all the bees."

It took some time, but that's just what he did. He ate up all the bees, every last one of them.

Then up he flew again to the Sultan's window.

"Cockadoodle-doo, Mister Sultana," he crowed. "Give me back my precious diamond!"

By now the Sultan was very tired, but he was still angry, very angry. He called in his servants. "After him!" he cried. "Catch me that cheeky rooster!"

So the Sultan's servants chased and chased the little red rooster until at last they caught him again.

"What am I going to do with him?" wailed the Sultan. "How am I ever going to get rid of him?" And he sat down in deep despair on his throne.

But just as he was sitting down, he happened to hear the cushions sighing and groaning underneath him, and that gave him a sudden and brilliant idea.

"Aha!" he cried, leaping to his feet. "You've definitely, definitely, definitely crowed your very last doodle-doo!"

"I don't think so, Mister Sultana," said the little red rooster.

"I've got you this time!" thundered the Sultan. "I'm going to sit on you! I'm going to squash you flat as a pancake. See how you like that!"

And he took the little red rooster by the neck and . . . and . . . and . . . stuffed him down the back of his capacious pantaloons. Then he sat down hard on him, very hard indeed.

But the little red rooster was not at all frightened of being squashed. He knew what to do about that. He simply said to himself: "Come, my full-up stomach. Come, my full up stomach, and let out all the bees. Let them sting the Sultan's bottom!"

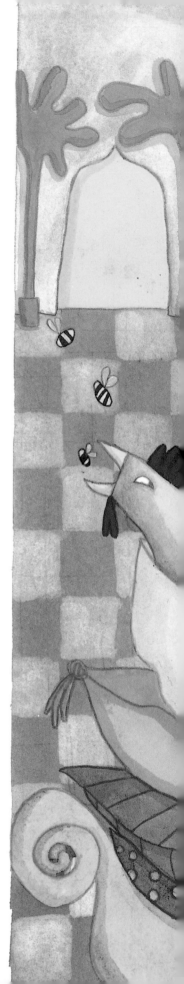

And that's just what he did. He let out all the
bees, every last one of them.

And did they sting the great almighty
Sultan's bottom? I should say so.

And did he screech and yowl and whimper?
I should say so.

And did the little red rooster hop out of those

capacious pantaloons, and fly away safe and sound? Well, of course he did.

"Cockadoodle-doo, Mister Sultana!" crowed the little red rooster. "Now, will you let me have my precious diamond?"

"AAEEE! OOOH! I give in," wailed the Sultan. "I give in. AAEEE! OOOH!"

So the Sultan's servants took the little red rooster up to the Sultan's bedchamber where the treasure chest was kept and gave him back his precious diamond.

"Now go!" they cried. "Shoo! Skidaddle!"

But the little red rooster did not go, not just yet. He had other ideas. The Sultan's servants had gone, and they had left the Sultan's treasure chest wide open. Rubies! Emeralds! Sapphires! Diamonds!

"Finders keepers!" thought the little red rooster. So he simply said: "Come, my empty stomach. Come, my empty stomach and gobble down all the Sultan's jewels."

It took some time, but that's just what he did. He gobbled down every last one of them.

Then off he went, back home to the little old widow. He had had quite enough of his adventures, quite enough of the big wide world. And, after all, he'd already found his fortune, hadn't he?

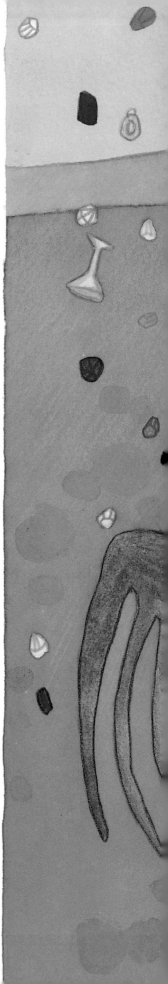

All night long he walked. It was morning by the time he got home and he was very tired.

"Cockadoodle-doo, Cockadoodle-doo," he crowed. "Let me in! Let me in!"

Out ran the little old widow at once.

"Where have you been, little red rooster?" she cried. "What have you been up to?"

"This and that," said the little red rooster. "This and that. But I'm home again, Mistress mine."

"I've been so worried about you," said the little old widow.

"Never will you have to worry again, Mistress mine," laughed the little red rooster. "Look what I have for you."

And he simply said to himself: "Come, my full-up stomach. Come, my full-up stomach and give up all you have."

cockadoodle-doo

Out onto the ground poured all the Sultan's jewels, every last one of them until there was a great sparkling pile of them at the poor old widow's feet. She sat down with a bump.

"Goodness me!" she cried. "Goodness me!"

"Cockadoodle-doo!" cried the little red rooster. "COCKADOODLE-DOO!"